The Next Door Friend

by Kim Kane
illustrated by Jon Davis

PICTURE WINDOW BOOKS
a capstone imprint

For my son, Edgar: working together to
redress the wanton lack of Edgars in fiction
(George, yours is on the way).

— *Kim*

Ginger Green is published by Picture Window Books,
A Capstone Imprint
1710 Roe Crest Drive
North Mankato, Minnesota 56003
www.mycapstone.com

Ginger Green, Playdate Queen — *The Next Door Friend*
Text Copyright © 2016 Kim Kane
Illustration Copyright © 2016 Jon Davis
Series Design Copyright © 2016 Hardie Grant Egmont
First published in Australia by Hardie Grant Egmont 2016

Library of Congress Cataloging-in-Publication Data
is available on the Library of Congress website.

978-1-5158-1949-3 (library binding)
978-1-5158-2011-6 (paperback)
978-1-5158-2017-8 (eBook PDF)
978-1-5158-2035-2 (reflowable epub)

Summary: Ginger loves to play with her neighbor, Edgar. But for some
reason, Edgar doesn't want to do anything Ginger wants to do. Can she
find something they both like to do?

Designers: Mack Lopez and Russell Griesmer
Production specialist: Tori Abraham

Printed and bound in China.
010737S18

Table of Contents

Chapter
One

My name is Ginger Green.

I am seven years old.

I am the Playdate Queen!

It is spring break. Today, Edgar is coming to my house.

Edgar is my new friend. He
just moved in next door.

Edgar does not go to my school.
He goes to a school just for boys.

I met Edgar on the street
this morning.

"How old are you?" I asked.

"I am seven," he said.

I said, "Edgar, I am Ginger Green, Playdate Queen.
We do not go to the same school, but we are both seven! Would you like to come and play with me later today?"

Edgar said,

"YES!"

At two o'clock, there is a KNOCK at the back door. I open the door.

"Hello!" says Edgar.

"What are you doing here?" I ask.

"You invited me over to play," says Edgar.

"But why are you at the back door?" I ask. "Visitors come in the front door."

"Not me," says Edgar. "I jumped over the fence."

"The fence is very tall," I say.

"That was brave!"

"I am like a robber," says Edgar.

"I jump over fences."

My little sister, Penny, comes into the kitchen.

"I am like a spider," says Edgar. "I always land on my feet."

"I am like a spider too," says Penny. "I am always naked."

Mom walks into the kitchen.
"Hello, Edgar," she says.
"Wow, you look just like
your mother."

"I am a **BOY**," says Edgar.
"I look like my **dad**."

Chapter
Two

"We are making a **cake**.
Would you like to stir?" I ask.

"No, thanks," says Edgar.
"Cooking is for girls."

"That is not true," I say.
"My dad cooks. And lots
of chefs on TV are boys."

"I don't like cooking," says Edgar.
"I like BOY things. I like sports."

Edgar takes a ball
from his pocket.

He **bounces** it.

He catches it.

He bounces it again.

Mom's lips make a straight line.

"No balls inside, Edgar."

Mom looks a bit **ANGRY**, so
I take Edgar to our room.

I share a room with my big sister, Violet. I turn on my music.

"Do you want to dance?" I ask. "I am Ginger Green, Disco Queen. You can be my Disco King."

"No, thanks," says Edgar. "Dancing is for girls."

"Dancing is not for girls,"
I say. "Lots of boys dance. At my
school, boys dance to hip-hop."

Edgar jumps up on Violet's bed.

"Not at my school," says Edgar.
"At my school, boys
play soccer."

Edgar JUMPS from Violet's bed to my bed.

"That was a BIG jump,"

I say.

"I am a pirate," says Edgar.
"I can JUMP from ship to
ship in high seas."

"Let's play pirates!"
I say.

"Actually, I would like to play soccer," says Edgar. "Let's go outside."

This is a **problem**. "We do not have a soccer ball," I say.

I am Ginger
Green, Playdate
Queen, and I
like dirt.

I am Ginger Green, Playdate
Queen, and I like jumping.

I like running.

I like dressing up,
and I like dancing.

I like Legos, and
I like cooking.

But I do not
like balls.
I cannot
catch them.

We walk outside. Edgar takes his ball from his pocket. He throws it to me.

I MISS IT.

Edgar throws the ball against the wall. It bounces back. He catches it. He throws it again. He catches it again. Edgar throws it to me.

I MISS.

I do not want to miss. I want to join in.

Edgar throws the ball against the wall. He catches it. He throws it again.

BAM!

I sit down.

I am in a **SLUMP**.
I am Ginger Green, Playdate
Queen, and on playdates,
I want to play. But I do
not want to play alone.

It is not a playdate if you play alone.

I want to play with Edgar.

Chapter
Three

I see my rope.

"Do you want to jump rope?"

I ask.

"I do not jump rope," says Edgar.

"Jumping rope is for girls."

"It is **not** for girls," I say loudly.
I am starting to feel angry.
"Jumping rope makes
you very fit. Even
soccer players
jump rope during
training to stay fit."

"Not at
my school,"

says Edgar.

Edgar throws his ball.

Edgar catches his ball.

Edgar pretends
to hold a trophy.

Edgar **cheers** loudly.

"What are you doing?"

I ask.

Edgar holds up his fingers in a **V** for victory. "I am a hero. An Olympic hero."

"Let's play pretend!" I say.

"Pretend is for girls,"

says Edgar.

I am very **angry** now. I am so angry that I am FURIOUS. Edgar is **wrong**. He is very wrong about what is for boys and what is for girls.

"Pretend is NOT for girls!" I shout.

"You are brave like a robber.

You land on your feet like a spider.

You jump ships like a pirate.

You do victory **V**s like a sports star. You are always pretending. And you are a boy."

"Yes. Yes, I am," Edgar says slowly. "I do like pretending."

"So let's pretend together," I say. "You can pretend things like robbers and pirates and spiders and sports stars. I will pretend things that I like. I like robbers and spiders, and I am already Ginger Green, Pirate Queen."

I pick up two sticks.
I give one to Edgar.

We fight like pirates.

We run around the backyard.
We dig for treasure.

We climb trees.

We make a pirate sail
for our pirate ship.

We look out for bad guys.

We play games, and we have fun.

Great fun.

Dad comes outside.

"Anyone want to lick the bowl?"

"I **LOVE** licking the bowl!" says Edgar.

I take a spoon. "I thought cooking was for girls?" I say.

"Licking the bowl is for boys and girls," says Edgar.

"It is not for boys, and it is not for girls," says Dad. "Licking the bowl is for dads."

Edgar laughs.

I am Ginger Green, Playdate
Queen. I like playing games that
boys think are for boys.

I like playing games that
girls think are for girls.

I like playing
most games.

I just don't
like balls.

I do like
playing with my
new friend Edgar.

I am happy he lives
next door.

THE END

About the
Author

Kim Kane

Kim Kane is an award-winning author who writes for children and teens in Australia and overseas. Kim's books include the CBCA short-listed picture book *Family Forest* and her middle-grade novel *Pip: the Story of Olive*. Kim lives with her family in Melbourne, Australia, and writes whenever and wherever she can.

About the Illustrator

Jon Davis

Pirates, old elephants, witches in bloomers, bears on bikes, ugly cats, sweet kids — Jon Davis does it all! Based in Twickenham, United Kingdom, Jon Davis has illustrated more than forty kids' books for publishers across the globe.

Collect them all!